The Storekeeper

The Storekeeper

GENERAL STORE

Tracey Campbell Pearson

Dial Books for Young Readers New York

Published by Dial Books for Young Readers
A Division of Penguin Books USA Inc.
375 Hudson Street
New York, New York 10014

Library of Congress Catalog Card Number: 87-36602
Printed in Hong Kong
First Pied Piper Printing 1991
ISBN 0-8037-1052-6
1 3 5 7 9 10 8 6 4 2

A Pied Piper Book is a registered trademark of
Dial Books for Young Readers,
a division of Penguin Books USA Inc.,
® TM 1,163,686 and ® TM 1,054,312.

THE STOREKEEPER
is also published in a hardcover edition by
Dial Books for Young Readers.

The art for each picture consists of an
ink, watercolor, and gouache painting that is
color-separated and reproduced in full color.

For the Dessos

Early, early every morning
while the rest of the town is still asleep

the storekeeper

starts her day.

It's time to open the store.

Good morning to the doughnut man,

to the road crew,

and to the sleepy children on their way to school.

All the town stops in

to say good morning!

The storekeeper has a busy day.

She must tidy her store

and sort the mail

while her customers look around.

Mrs. Bond buys a lot. Miss Dickerson, a little.

Hank from the road crew stops by to say hello.

Salespeople bring her fancy things from far away

and special things from right next door.

The storekeeper buys what she thinks

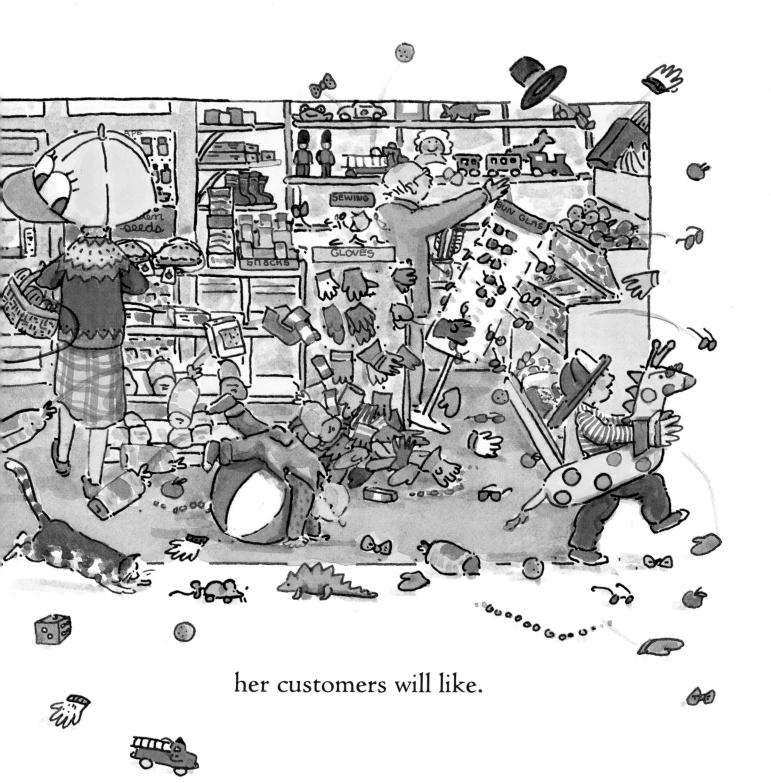

her customers will like.

Evening finally arrives.

Still her customers come and go

until late at night,

when her work is done,

and the storekeeper says

to all the town

good night!